D0118652

Jackson
County
Library
System

FINZEL THE FARSIGHTED

by Paul Fleischman

illustrated by Marcia Sewall

A Unicorn Book   E. P. Dutton   New York

Library of Congress Cataloging in Publication Data

Fleischman, Paul.
  Finzel the farsighted.

  Summary: Although his nearsightedness causes
difficulties, Finzel the Farsighted is blessed with
the ability to see into the future.
  [1. Fortune telling—Fiction]   I. Sewall, Marcia, ill.
II. Title.
PZ7.F599233Fi   1983   83-1416
ISBN 0-525-44057-7

Published in the United States by E. P. Dutton, Inc.,
2 Park Avenue, New York, N.Y. 10016

Published simultaneously in Canada by Clarke,
Irwin & Company Limited, Toronto and Vancouver

Editor: Emilie McLeod   Designer: Isabel Warren-Lynch

Printed in the U.S.A.   First Edition
10 9 8 7 6 5 4 3 2 1

Was there ever a stronger man? Surely.

A more passionate suitor? No doubt.

But a man richer in wisdom? Never! For before the gaze of Finzel the Farsighted, the fortune-teller of the village of Plov, the secrets of the universe opened like blossoms in spring.

He could see deep into a baker's past simply by reading a slice of his bread. He could probe far into a cooper's future merely by knocking on his barrels and listening. If you worked as a scribe, he might peer into your ink bottle and tell you of a flea bite that wasn't due for thirty years, describing its size, its shape, its location —and the subsequent history of the flea.

And yet, although his enormous learning allowed
him to glimpse the past and the future, Finzel's eyes
were so poor that he often had trouble making out
the present. He once set carrots in his candlesticks
by mistake and tried to light them with a fishbone
which he took for a match. He would leave his dirty
clothes at the cobbler's to be washed and his worn-
out shoes at the washerwoman's. One year he even
mistook the crop of plums on his tree for a flock of

blackbirds—and spent the entire summer trying his best to scare them away.

Finzel lived alone. He was round as a pumpkin and had a great gray beard that fanned out over his belly. His appetite was astounding, and each day he crowded his dining room table with baskets of fruit, whole circles of cheese, plates of meat, saucers of soup, jam pots, wine bottles, and whatever else he had in the house for his immense midday meal.

Early one summer afternoon, just as Finzel was sitting down to eat, there came a knock at the door. It was Pavel, the village simpleton, his head of blond hair sticking out in every direction like a feather duster.

"I'd like you to read my fortune," he said. He reached deep into a pocket and brought out a lemon he'd picked from his tree.

Finzel studied it curiously—and recognized it at last.

"But of course, a lemon! A most eloquent fruit. Come, Pavel, and join me for dinner, and then let us see what it has to say." He placed the lemon on the dining room table, where it disappeared among the food, and the two men sat down to eat.

It happened, however, that there was another lemon besides Pavel's on the table that day. It had been grown by a sickly old woman named Mashka, a fruit seller who'd sold it to Finzel that morning, coughing and sneezing all the while. Forgetting which lemon he was supposed to save, Finzel grabbed Pavel's in the course of the meal, cut it in two with a carving knife, and squeezed it into a cup of tea. While Pavel was absorbed with eating a meat pie, Finzel drained the cup with one gulp and moved on to a plate of salmon.

❧ 8 ❧

When the meal was finished, Finzel cleared the table,
leaving nothing but Mashka's lemon and a knife.

"You're certain you grew this lemon?" he asked.

"Certain," Pavel replied.

Carefully, Finzel cut it in two. His brows were
furrowed with concentration as he peered into one half
and then the other, squinting as though looking through
a keyhole. He noted the bumps on the lemon's surface.

He considered its shape. He sniffed at its skin. He removed the seeds and examined them closely. At last he put the lemon down.

"Tell me, Pavel—have you been coughing a lot?"

Pavel's heart began to gain speed.

"In truth, I hadn't noticed," he replied. "But now that you mention it—I believe you're right." He squirmed about nervously in his chair.

"I don't wish to worry you," said Finzel, "but I'm afraid you're not in the best of health."

Pavel's eyes opened wide. He hands began trembling.

"The lemon shows plainly that last Tuesday night you had the misfortune to come down with a cold—one that will take hold like a leech, it appears. If I were you, I'd run straightaway home, jump into bed, and stay there."

Pavel's whole body began to shake. Though young and in the best of health, no sooner had he heard the fortune-teller's words than he began to imagine himself ripe for the grave. Springing to his feet, he thanked Finzel profusely, put a coin on the table, and rushed out the door.

"That my lungs have never been good is no secret," he muttered to himself as he hurried along. "And my heart—why it's hardly strong enough to keep a gnat in the air. Mother herself said I was small as a baby—and frail as a butterfly besides!"

Though it was only a short walk back to his house, Pavel arrived panting and wheezing, as though he'd climbed a mountain. His thieving brother Osip, who lived next door and was sly as Pavel was simple, saw him trudging by from his porch.

"Dear brother!" he called out with mock concern. "What's the matter? You look exhausted!" He spat out a mouthful of seeds from a watermelon he'd just stolen from Pavel's garden.

"How else should I look," Pavel replied, "considering the state of my health!" And with that, he flung open his door, dove into bed, and fell asleep.

A few days later, Finzel called on Mashka to buy
some nuts. The old woman's skin was pale as skimmed
milk. Her teeth chattered furiously, and her lips were
blue. Great fits of coughing doubled her over like a
marionette taking a bow.

"That cold of mine's vanished completely," she joked
while the fortune-teller inspected her walnuts. "It turned
into the whooping cough instead."

That afternoon Pavel returned to Finzel to see if his prospects had improved. He shuffled along through the stifling heat and arrived just as Finzel was sitting down to eat. He brought with him a walnut from one of his trees.

"Ah yes, the walnut," Finzel declared. "An encyclopedia of information—and delectable as well." He set it down on the dining room table and invited Pavel to join him.

It happened, however, that scattered among the dishes lay a pound of walnuts that Finzel had bought from Mashka that morning. While Pavel was intent on a bowl of baked apples, Finzel cracked Pavel's walnut by mistake, gobbled it up, and turned his attention to the roast goose.

When the meal was finished, Finzel cleared the table, leaving nothing but one of Mashka's walnuts.

"You're sure that this came from your tree?" he asked.

Pavel coughed weakly and nodded.

Finzel cracked the walnut between his palms and extracted the nutmeat whole. He weighed it in his hand, ran his fingers over its bumps, and examined it from every angle like a gemstone. At last he set it down and sighed.

"I'm afraid, dear Pavel, that you're a very sick man."

Pavel gaped at Finzel in awe and felt his hands begin to quiver.

"That cold of yours has grown into whooping cough—and it appears that won't be the end of it. If I

were you, I'd hurry back home, bundle myself up in a blanket, and keep a fire going day and night."

Pavel hastily thanked the fortune-teller, paid for his visit, and left.

"So it's whooping cough!" he said to himself. "Just as I suspected all along. For days my forehead's been hot as a teakettle, and these hands of mine—shaking like leaves! As if it weren't enough to have this pain in my chest, and all with a heart that couldn't push a worm through the ground!"

Though he was covered with sweat from the heat of the day, Pavel lit a fire as soon as he got home, wrapped himself up in a woolen blanket, and brought his rocking chair up close to the stove. A few minutes later, Osip stopped by.

"Dear brother! What are you doing bundled up like a baby on a day like this?"

Pavel scooted his chair even closer to the stove. "You're speaking, Osip, to a *very* sick man. Finzel the Farsighted has said so himself. I'm fading, brother—fading fast."

"But you're only twenty years old!" replied Osip. "You've always been as healthy as a horse, and strong as a bear besides."

"All that has changed, I'm sorry to say. Now please be so good as to fetch me more wood. And then, I'm afraid, I shall need to rest."

Chuckling over his brother's lunacy, Osip brought in more wood from the shed and decided to accompany Pavel on his next trip to the fortune-teller.

One morning, several days later, Finzel paid Mashka another visit to buy some fresh vegetables. The old woman looked worse than ever. Her eyes were watering, and she shook with the chills. Her nose ran like a leaky faucet, and she sneezed loudly into a big red handkerchief.

"That whooping cough finally disappeared," she said while the fortune-teller surveyed the tomatoes. "It's pneumonia I've got now."

That afternoon, just as Finzel was preparing to sit down and eat, Pavel and Osip knocked at the door. Pavel had with him a head of lettuce from his garden.

"But of course, the worthy lettuce," said Finzel. "A most informative vegetable—and so very delicious as well." He set it down on the dining room table and asked his two guests to join him.

It happened, however, that near the raspberry tarts and the leg of lamb lay another head of lettuce, which Finzel had bought from Mashka that morning. Forgetting which was which, Finzel reached for Pavel's lettuce, bit into it as if it were an apple, and devoured it between sips of beet soup. Though Pavel was concentrating on a leg of turkey, Osip saw exactly what happened.

When the meal was finished, Finzel cleared the table, leaving only Mashka's head of lettuce.

"You're certain you grew this yourself?" he asked.

Feebly, Pavel nodded his head.

Finzel carefully picked up the lettuce and gently peeled off leaf after leaf. He examined each one minutely, nodding here, raising an eyebrow there, as though he were reading a book. The head of lettuce gradually grew smaller. Finally he removed the last leaf, studied it, and set it down.

"By this time I don't have to tell you, Pavel, that you're not at all a well man. In truth, last Wednesday you came down with pneumonia."

Pavel froze, staring into space.

"Unfortunately, a bug gnawed one of the leaves, and I'm unable to tell whether you'll recover. But if I were you, I'd watch my health as closely as a hen watches her chicks."

Slowly Pavel rose to his feet. Dropping a coin on the table, he thanked Finzel with the voice of a ghost and shuffled out the door with Osip.

"Pneumonia!" he muttered, as if in a trance. "Well, brother, when Death calls, there's no pretending you're deaf. I'll arrange to have a will made up tomorrow. And if you'd let me bestow on you my few possessions, I'd be deeply honored."

"And I, dear brother, should be *honored* to accept them." He entered his house, scoffing at the fortune-teller.

"Finzel the Farsighted, indeed!" he muttered. Why the fool was as blind as a mole in the ground—so blind that he read the wrong fortunes by mistake. And a *wealthy* fool he was at that—wealthy enough to eat like a king.

Suddenly Osip's eyes lit up. He hopped to his feet and began pacing about. How could he have overlooked such a gold mine before? What could be simpler than robbing a man who couldn't tell one head of lettuce from another? The only thing he had to do was to learn where Finzel kept his money—and at once an idea leapt into his mind.

Late that night, while the village slept, Osip snuck down to Finzel's house, plucked a poppy from his window box, and scurried back home again.

The next morning he knocked on Finzel's door, disguised in an overcoat and carrying a cane, with a wide-brimmed hat pulled over his eyes.

"Thank heavens you're home!" Osip exclaimed when Finzel opened the door. "Is it true that your eyes can see the past and the future?"

"That is correct," Finzel replied.

"Bless you, sir!" Osip cried out. "All the way from Vilsk, I've come—and now, at least, I shall have the answer!" He pulled Finzel's poppy from his pocket and handed it to the fortune-teller.

"The poppy, of course," Finzel remarked. "So very instructive—and beautiful besides. You grew the flower yourself, did you?"

"Naturally," Osip replied.

The two men sat down at a table. Gently handling the closed-up poppy, Finzel carefully unwound the petals until the flower stood open.

"You see," said Osip, "I'm a wealthy man."

Finzel peered into the flower like a bee. "So I see in the poppy here," he replied.

"And just to be safe, you understand, I hide my money somewhere new every week. The problem is that I've completely forgotten where in the world I last put it!"

Finzel studied the poppy with care. "It appears that you have it inside a strongbox."

"Yes, of course—in a strongbox!" Osip burst out. "And I've placed the strongbox—"

"Under the bed."

"Why, yes, that's right! Under the bed! And the key to the strongbox is—"

"Under your pillow."

"But of course—under my pillow!" cried Osip. "How very stupid of me."

Osip smiled with satisfaction. Then all of a sudden he had an idea. Since Finzel was able to read the fu-

ture, why not make sure that he wouldn't be caught?

Osip looked over at the fortune-teller. "I'm most grateful, sir. I'd be a pauper without you. But there's one further matter, I'm afraid. For in spite of all the precautions I've taken, I've been troubled by a feeling that I'm going to be robbed."

Finzel examined the stem of the poppy. "You will indeed—and this very night."

"Good Lord!" cried Osip. "And the rogue—will he escape?"

Finzel slowly shook out some pollen and studied it in silence. "On the contrary," he declared. "The thief will be caught."

Osip abruptly sat up in his chair. Caught? He swallowed and glanced about. He'd best not go through with it after all.

"That is," said Finzel, "*one* thief will be caught. Tonight you'll be robbed not once, but twice."

Twice! Osip nervously shuffled his feet. Someone else must be after this idiot's gold!

"The first thief will escape," continued Finzel. "But the second will meet up with justice, I promise you."

Osip smiled—and decided to make sure he was first in line to steal the man's money. He rose and thanked the fortune-teller, gave him a coin which he planned to reclaim, and walked out the door with the help of his cane.

That evening, as soon as the sun had set, Osip crept toward Finzel's house, determined to be the first of the two thieves. Patiently, he waited behind a tree. He watched as Finzel's lamp went out, allowed him time to fall asleep, then climbed inside through a window.

From the bedroom came the sound of snoring. Moving as silently as a spider, Osip inched his way toward the door.

Suddenly a mouse carrying a morsel of bread shot out of the kitchen and darted past Osip, startling him so that he bumped a table and caused a pitcher to shatter on the floor.

Instantly Osip froze in his tracks. Finzel's snoring came to a halt, and all of a sudden the house was silent. Osip's heart pounded. His palms were sweating. He stood perfectly still, not daring to move.

Finally Osip caught the sound of Finzel's familiar snore. Creeping stealthily into the bedroom, he slid his hand under Finzel's pillow and grasped an iron key. Then he opened the strongbox he found under the bed, pulled out a pillowcase full of coins, and climbed back out the window.

"How I pity the second thief!" Osip chuckled. "To find nothing to steal—and be caught in the bargain!" He dashed along the road toward his house, cackling with delight.

In the morning, Finzel got out of bed—and gaped in shock at the empty strongbox.

"Robbed!" he cried. "Robbed and ruined!" Who, he thought, will come to a fortune-teller who couldn't foresee his own robbery? And if the thief isn't caught—what then? He'd be the laughingstock of the village of Plov!

Then an idea flew into Finzel's head. Without mentioning the theft, he'd offer to read all the villagers' fortunes, for free. No matter how the scoundrel might try to hide it, the theft would show up in his past—and Finzel would have his thief.

He started immediately at one end of Plov and worked his way toward the other. He tossed up a handful of the miller's flour and watched it drift away on the breeze. He rolled one of the wheelwright's wheels down a path and pondered the course it took. He listened to the ticking of the clockmaker's clocks. He studied the surface of the blacksmith's anvil. But nowhere did he find what he was looking for.

At last Finzel came to Pavel's house and found Osip there, visiting his brother.

"Dear Osip, good afternoon to you. Nursing your brother, I see, and with great devotion I'm sure. I interrupt only to ask if you and Pavel would like to have your fortunes read, free."

Osip was struck speechless, realizing he might be caught. Then suddenly a plan sprang to mind.

"Why certainly! We should be only too happy." He dashed out to Pavel's garden and pulled out one of his onions. Then he ran over to his own garden and pulled out one of his own.

"Here's one of Pavel's onions," he told Finzel, handing the fortune-teller his own. "And here is one just pulled from my own garden." He handed Finzel Pavel's onion.

"Excellent," said Finzel, placing the onions in his pocket. Then he caught sight of Pavel, lying in his bed, and quietly approached.

"I'm headed for the grave," whispered Pavel, "as sure as the sun's headed west. As for the funeral—nothing fancy, please. Just cover me up and leave me in peace."

Sadly, Finzel gazed down at Pavel. Then he found a knife and sat down beside him. Forgetting which was which, he reached in his pocket, pulled out the onion that Pavel had grown, and carefully sliced it in two.

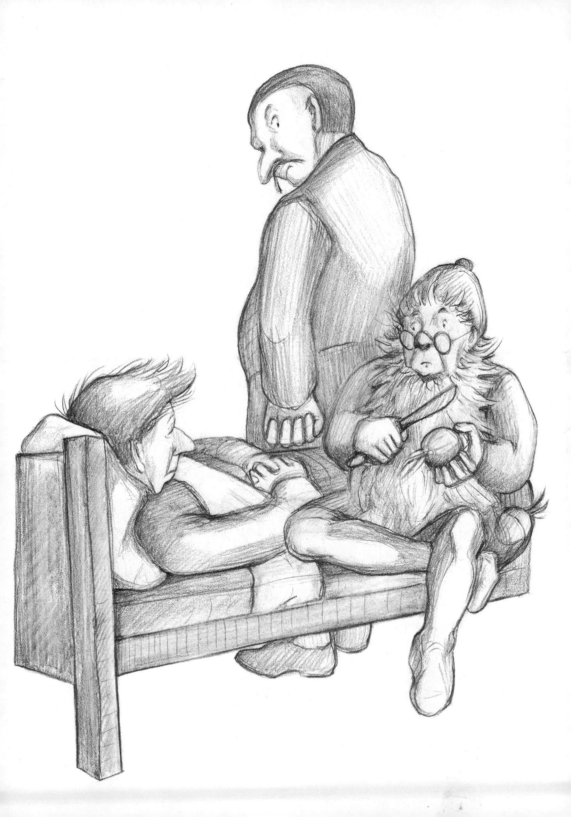

His eyebrows jerked upward when he saw the pattern of rings that had been revealed. He bent over the onion, studying it in awe—and all of a sudden jumped to his feet.

"A miracle!" he cried.

"What is it?" asked Osip.

"Pavel's pneumonia!" Finzel exclaimed. "It appears to have vanished without a trace!"

Like a sprung trap, Pavel sat up in bed.

"*Vanished?*" he asked in disbelief.

"Completely," Finzel declared. "You're a new man entirely—the very model of health. Why, you've still got eighty-five years to live, and without so much as a sneeze!"

"A new man, you say," Pavel whispered. He took a long, deep breath and stretched his arms like a man arising from the dead. "And the very model of health, at that!"

He flung back the covers, leapt out of bed, threw on his clothes, and rushed out the door, anxious to get back to work on his garden.

"Never have I seen a man cured so quickly," Finzel addressed Osip while slicing the other onion. Then suddenly his eyebrows shot up.

"The thief!" he burst out, eyeing the onion.

Terror-stricken, Osip froze. The fool, he realized, must have mixed up the onions—and gotten them right by mistake!

"Written right here in the rings!" shouted Finzel.

Wondering how he could possibly be caught since he was the first thief to reach Finzel's house, Osip dashed for dear life out the door—straight into the arms of Gregor the jailer.

"Seize him!" yelled Finzel.

Gregor, who'd heard fortunes were being read for free and had sought out Finzel for fear of missing out, handcuffed Osip in an instant. The three of them walked over to Osip's house, where Finzel found his money in a soup kettle.

"Thank goodness!" the fortune-teller exclaimed. Gregor tightened his grip on Osip and prepared to lead him off to jail.

"One question, please, Finzel," Osip spoke up. "Were you not robbed by *two* different thieves last night?"

Finzel fingered his long gray beard.

"As a matter of fact I was," he replied. "The other villain escaped, unfortunately. Luckily, nothing of value was taken—a bit of cheese, a little bread. Probably nothing more than a mouse."

And Finzel the Farsighted walked cheerfully home.